Magic
Animal Friends

For Paige and Will Standish

Special thanks to Valerie Wilding

ORCHARD BOOKS

First published in Great Britain in 2017 by The Watts Publishing Group

1 3 5 7 9 10 8 6 4 2

Text copyright © Working Partners Ltd 2017
Illustrations copyright © Working Partners Ltd 2017
Series created by Working Partners Ltd

A CIP catalogue record for this book is available from the British Library.

ISBN 978 1 40836 079 8

Printed in Great Britain

Orchard Books
An imprint of Hachette Children's Group
Part of The Watts Publishing Group Limited
Carmelite House, 50 Victoria Embankment, London EC4Y 0DZ

An Hachette UK Company
www.hachette.co.uk
www.hachettechildrens.co.uk

Layla Brighteye
Keeps a Lookout

Daisy Meadows

ORCHARD

Brighteyes' Home

Spelltop School

Treehouse

Picnic Area

Twinkling Inkwell

Sunshine Meadow

Honey Tree

Map of Friendship Forest

Library

Playground

Greenhouse

School Hall

Madame Doodleflap's House

Can you keep a secret? I thought you could!

Then I'll tell you about an enchanted wood.

It lies through the door in the old oak tree,

Let's go there now - just follow me!

We'll find adventure that never ends,

And meet the Magic Animal Friends!

Love,
Goldie the Cat

Contents

CHAPTER ONE

Painting Parrots

"Look at Giggles go!" Jess Forester said to her best friend, Lily Hart. "He doesn't stay still for a moment, does he?"

Giggles the parrot was flying around an aviary, an enormous cage made of wire netting and wood. It was part of Helping Paw Wildlife Hospital, which Lily's

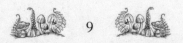

parents ran inside the barn close by. Both girls adored helping to care for the poorly animals. As well as Giggles, the aviary contained a duck with a damaged wing, who was nibbling at some lettuce, and two young pigeons. They were cooing sleepily in the autumn sunshine, their heads gently resting together.

While Lily went into the aviary to fill up water bowls for the birds, Jess tried to paint Giggles. She had her paints and sketchbook spread out on the grass in front of her. Jess squirted some yellow and blue paint into a pot, and mixed them together with her paintbrush to make green. Giggles flashed by in a blur of green feathers. A white bandage was tied around his foot.

"He's going to be hard to paint, flying around like that," said Lily. "Are you going to paint his bandage too?"

Jess held up the paint pot, frowning. "I need to mix the right colour for his feathers first," she said. "This green doesn't look bright enough."

Giggles shot past again. "Bedtime!" he squawked. "Bedtime, Giggles!"

Lily grinned. "My dad said parrots copy what they hear people say. I bet his owner says 'Bedtime' to him every night!"

"Night, Giggles!" the parrot squawked. "Night, night!"

Both girls laughed.

"I love it when he talks," said Jess. "Do you know what it reminds me of?"

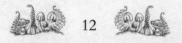

"Friendship Forest!" said Lily, with a trill of excitement.

Friendship Forest was a secret magical world where all the animals lived in little cottages, and visited the Toadstool Café for honey buns and hazelnut cream milkshakes. Best of all, they could talk! The girls' special friend, Goldie the cat, often took them to the forest, where they'd had lots of amazing adventures.

Giggles settled on a perch, put his head on one side and squawked, "Hello!"

"Hello!" Jess called back.

But Giggles looked past her. "Kitty!

 13

Kitty! Kitty!" he squawked.

"What kitty?" Lily wondered as she stepped out of the aviary.

Jess glanced around. A golden cat, with eyes as green as Giggles's feathers, was running across the grass.

"Goldie!" Jess cried.

The beautiful cat bounded over. The girls stroked her as she rubbed against their legs and purred. Lily grinned.

"She's come to

take us to Friendship Forest for another adventure!"

Goldie turned and ran towards Brightley Stream, at the bottom of the garden. The girls followed, hearts racing with excitement. Since no time passed while they were in Friendship Forest, they knew their parents wouldn't worry about them.

Goldie led them over the stepping stones across the stream, then through Brightley Meadow towards an old, bare tree. As Goldie reached it, red, orange and yellow autumn leaves burst from its branches. A woodpecker scurried up the trunk. Bright goldfinches swooped down to peck seeds from thistles growing in the lush grass below. A butterfly perched on an orange toadstool, flexing her wings.

When the girls caught up, Goldie touched the tree with her paw. Words formed in the bark, and together the girls excitedly read them aloud. "Friendship Forest!"

A door appeared in the trunk. Jess's eyes sparkled as she turned the leaf-shaped handle. Golden light spilled out and Goldie leaped inside.

The girls followed her into the golden glow, and felt themselves tingle all over. They knew that meant they were shrinking, just a little.

When the light faded, they found themselves in Friendship Forest. Birdsong rang through the treetops and the air was scented by candyfloss flowers. Goldie stood upright beside them, wearing her glittering scarf. She pulled the girls into a warm hug.

"It's lovely to have you back in Friendship Forest!" Goldie said to the girls in her soft voice.

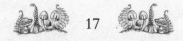

"It's lovely to be here!" said Jess.

"But why have you brought us to the forest, Goldie?" Lily asked. "I hope Grizelda's not causing trouble again."

Grizelda was a bad witch who desperately wanted Friendship Forest for herself. She was always trying to drive the animals away. The girls had managed to stop her so far but she kept coming back.

"She's not at Spelltop School again, is she?" Jess added.

Spelltop School was where the youngest Friendship Forest animals went to learn. On Lily and Jess's last adventure,

Grizelda and her flamingo helpers had plotted to steal magical books from the school library. Grizelda had tried to turn the books' good magic into bad witchy magic, but Goldie and the girls made sure that didn't happen.

Goldie shook her head. "Spelltop needs your help again, but for a good reason this time." Her ears pricked up. "Listen!"

Jingle jangle! Jingle jangle!

"That's the school bluebell ringing," said Goldie. She took the girls' hands in her paws. "Come on! We're off to Spelltop School!"

CHAPTER TWO

Professor Gogglewing's Book

The friends hurried through the forest, passing flowers of every colour. Delicious scents of chocolate, lemon and strawberry wafted from their petals. Soon they reached Spelltop School. Brightly painted picnic tables stood around the grassy playground, which had rope swings and a treehouse. There was a seesaw, too, made from a plank balanced over a huge log. Somewhere a class was singing:

"*Mice and voles, come out and play,*

The sun has chased the rain away …"

Lily opened the yellow gate that led

into the school. Caught on the latch was a shred of black cloth. "Someone's torn their clothes," Lily said. She unhooked the bit of cloth – and her nose wrinkled as she caught a whiff of something horrible. "Yuck! It stinks of mouldy socks and rotten eggs!"

Goldie sniffed. "It smells like Grizelda's magic sparks."

"And it looks like her horrid cloak!" said Jess. She groaned. "Don't say she's been lurking around."

"Honk!"

An elderly goose wearing spectacles

waddled towards them with a book tucked beneath his wing. His blue waistcoat was dotted with pockets. A pen poked out of one, and a banana from another.

"Professor Gogglewing!" said Goldie.

"Good morning, everyone!" said the goose. "The top class have art today. They're doing portraits, and I asked them to choose someone to paint – someone who they admired. Jess and Lily, they chose you! Do say you'll pose for them!"

The girls grinned. "We'd love to!"

"Wonderful!" said Professor

Gogglewing.
He took
them to
the art room,
where lots of
young animals sat at easels.

"It's Lily and Jess!" whispered Lulu
Flufftail the squirrel. Her tail bristled with
excitement.

Penny and Jenny Nibblesqueak the
hamsters waved. They had pastry crumbs
down their fronts, which the girls guessed
must have come from the buns sold at
their family's bakery.

 25

"Hello everyone!" said Lily and Jess.

Just then, the store cupboard door opened. Out came a lovely fluffy white cat wearing a pink bow.

"Professor Cutiepaws!" Jess cried in delight.

The cat's deep blue eyes widened in surprise. She dropped the pot she was carrying, spilling orange paint all over her fluffy white fur.

"Oh, bouncing

blossoms!" she cried in alarm, and darted back into the cupboard.

The girls smiled. Professor Cutiepaws was clumsy, but nice.

A moment later, she reappeared. To the girls' astonishment, her fur was spotless.

"Wow!" said Jess. "She must have magical cleaning wipes!"

"Silly ickle me!" said Professor Cutiepaws. "I was just surprised to see you two girlies! Pleasantly surprised, of course."

Professor Gogglewing honked. "Jess and Lily say you can paint them," he

announced to the class.

"Hooray!" the class cheered. Professor Cutiepaws clapped her fluffy white paws in delight.

"But first," said Professor Gogglewing, "look at this!" He held up the book he'd been carrying. It had a picture of Spelltop School on the cover.

"It's called *The Colours of Friendship Forest* and it's very precious," he said, "so it's not usually allowed out of the library. But Professor Cutiepaws asked if she could borrow it to teach you all about colour."

 28

He opened the book at a beautiful
woodland scene. "The pictures were
painted by the greatest artist ever
known in Friendship Forest – Madame
Doodleflap!"

A little meerkat pup bobbed up. "Wow!"
she squealed. She had a light
brown coat with silvery
stripes, a dainty pointed
nose and dark, shining
eyes. "I love Madame
Doodleflap's paintings. Can
I see? Can I? Can I?"

She scampered over

and Professor Gogglewing gave her the book.

Jess crouched beside her. "I love paintings, too," she said. "My name's Jess."

"I'm Layla Brighteye," said the meerkat. "Madame Doodleflap's my favourite artist, and Mum says if I practise hard, I could paint like her one day. Do you think I will? Do you?"

Jess laughed. "I'm sure you will!"

Professor Gogglewing left the classroom and Professor Cutiepaws began handing out paper.

Lily kneeled beside Layla as she turned

the pages. "Here's a picture of Toadstool Glade," she said.

"And there's Sunshine Meadow," said Jess.

"And the Treasure Tree," said Goldie, pointing to a painting of the tree, which grew all sorts of foods the animals needed.

"I'd love to ask Madame Doodleflap how she mixes her colours," said Jess. "I've

been struggling to get the right green for a painting."

"You can't ask her," said Layla sadly. "No one's ever met her. We don't even know where she lives!"

"Sweetiepies, we're ready to begin!" Professor Cutiepaws called in her high voice.

The girls took up their poses at the front of the class. Lily sat with a book, posing as if she was reading. Jess stood, pretending to wave to someone. All the animals were studying them closely and the girls caught each other's eyes. It was hard to stay still and not giggle!

While the pupils painted, Professor Cutiepaws tidied the store cupboard. The only sound was the soft swish of brushes.

But soon Jess and Lily noticed a new sound – a grumbly one. It came from the corner of the room, where all they could see was a pair of enormous sunglasses peering over an easel.

The grumbles became louder. "Should be

painting me … Everyone would love a picture of me …"

Crash!

The animal's easel fell over, and a pink flamingo stood up on long, thin legs. "I'll show them!" he cried.

Then he flapped his wings, flew across the classroom and grabbed the book of paintings. The weight made him wobble, and his sunglasses slipped off.

Jess gasped. It was one of Grizelda's helpers. "Gonzo!" she cried.

Lily's hands flew to her mouth. "Oh no! This means trouble!"

CHAPTER THREE

Clumsy Professor Cutiepaws

Gonzo flapped around high above the class. The little animals scattered as Lily and Jess clambered over chairs, trying to get the book back from him.

Professor Cutiepaws bounded on to a desk. "Stand back, honeybunches!" she

 35

cried. "I'll get the book!"

As Gonzo swooped low over her, she
jumped up and grabbed it.

"Well done, Professor Cutiepaws!" cried
Jess. "Watch out – he might try to steal it
back from you!"

But Gonzo didn't.
He grabbed his
sunglasses from
where they'd fallen on
the ground and flew away
out of the window.

Professor Cutiepaws

jumped off the desk. She staggered a little, almost dropping the book. It fell open, and Professor Cutiepaws struggled clumsily to close it. Her paws flew to and fro as she flipped the pages.

Layla tried to help, but Professor Cutiepaws snapped the book shut and said, "Thank you, sweetie. I've got it safe and sound."

But just then she turned – and slipped! The book went flying, straight towards the sink. It was full of water for washing up paint pots.

Splash!

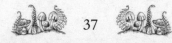

Jess rushed to fish the book out. It was dripping wet – and the drops were coloured blue, green, yellow …

Lily pointed to the cover of the book, where the picture of Spelltop School had begun to melt away like an ice cream on a hot day. "The picture's washing off!" she cried.

Jess opened the book and flipped frantically through the white pages. "They're all blank!" she said in dismay. "All the colours have washed away!"

"Boo hoo hoo!" sobbed Professor Cutiepaws, covering her eyes with her

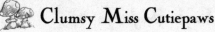

paws. They heard frightened whispers from the animals.

Lily looked up to see that the cheerful blue of the classroom walls had begun to fade. Jenny Nibblesqueak's red headband was turning a horrible greyish-pink!

"What's happening?" Penny Nibblesqueak cried, pointing to her sister.

"My paint colours have gone peculiar!" wailed Lucy Longwhiskers the bunny.

"I'm such a butterfingers!" wept

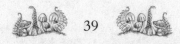

Professor Cutiepaws in dismay. "I mean, butterpaws! It's all my fault."

Lily comforted her. "No, it's not. Grizelda must have sent Gonzo to grab the book. I bet she put a spell on it … somehow."

"That's right!" said Jess. She glanced around. Everything in the room was turning the same sludgy colour.

"Grizelda must have used her horrible magic to make the colours wash away from the forest too," said Goldie. "But how? She isn't here."

"Boo hoo hoo!" Professor Cutiepaws

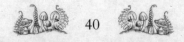

snuffled. "I'm such a silly billy sausage. If only I hadn't dropped the book."

Lily patted the cat's fluffy paw. "Don't worry. We'll find a way to put this right."

"Oh, I don't know if you should," said Professor Cutiepaws. "I don't want anyone to be in any danger."

"Let's ask Professor Wiggly the librarian to help," said Jess. "He fixed the potions book after Grizelda used magic on it."

Layla the little meerkat bobbed up. "I'm coming, too! I want to help bring the colours back."

Lottie Littlestripe the badger pointed her paw at the window. "Oh, no!" she moaned.

Lily followed her gaze. To everyone's horror, the lush green treetops were slowly fading. So were the blossoms scrambling over the library roof.

"Everything is losing its colours!" Lily said.

The little animals began to cry.

"Our lovely forest!" sobbed Lulu Flufftail.

"The pretty flowers!" squeaked Dolly
Twinkletail the mouse.

"They'll all be spoiled," Lucy
Longwhiskers whimpered.

Professor Cutiepaws dabbed her eyes.
"Oh dearie me," she said. "Grizelda has

won with her clever plan." She sniffed.
"Who'd want to live somewhere with no
colours? All the poor ickle animals will
have to leave the forest."

"We won't let that happen!" said Jess.
"Lily, Goldie! We have to get help – fast!"

CHAPTER FOUR

The Mysterious Madame Doodleflap

Goldie, Layla and the girls darted across
the playground and into the library.

They all gasped. Everything inside
was bright and cheery. The books on the
shelves were green and orange and purple.
The cosy nooks where animals could curl

 45

up to read still had red cushions and blue armchairs.

"Of course!" said Lily. "Professor Wiggly put a charm on the library so witches can't come in. Witchy magic doesn't work here!"

Professor Wiggly the bookworm was stretched along a section of books labelled "Forest Flowers", dusting them with a turquoise peacock feather. He sang as he worked.

"Nice and clean, clean and nice,

You'll be sparkling in a trice."

"Hello, Professor!" Goldie called.

Professor Wiggly looked around, beaming. "Hello, everyone! Lovely to see you!" He shimmied tail first down a ladder, then wiggled over to the friends. "How can I help?"

"Look at this book, Professor," said Jess, handing it over.

He examined it. "Oh my! It's blank!"

Lily explained what had happened.

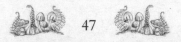

"We think Grizelda somehow put a spell on it," she finished. "Now the forest is losing its colours too!"

Professor Wiggly wiggled to the window. He gasped. "What dreadful magic! The poor forest!"

Layla went over to him. "But you know how to fix it, don't you, Professor?" she asked anxiously.

"I'm sorry, but I can't," said the bookworm. "There's only one way to put colour back into our forest. The pictures must be painted again. Madame Doodleflap did the original ones, so she's the only person who can repaint them."

"But nobody knows where she lives," said Layla.

Goldie's whiskers drooped. "Can't we think of a way to find her?"

Professor Wiggly closed his eyes in thought, and Layla buried her face in her paws. Goldie stared at the ceiling, and the girls racked their brains.

Suddenly Layla bobbed up, her eyes sparkling. "I know! Why don't we look at Madame Doodleflap's paintings? Nobody has seen her, so she must paint close to her home. Maybe we can look at her paintings and work out where her home must be."

"It's a great idea," Lily said gently. "But all her paintings were washed away."

Layla bounced up and down. "I've got some – at home, stuck up in my bedroom! Come on, I'll show you."

"Take the book," Professor Wiggly said. "You'll need to keep it close to you if you're going to save our forest."

"Thanks, Professor!" they cried.

The four friends ran outside and stared in horror at the trees. Nearly all the leaves had turned a horrible grey.

"If we don't hurry," Lily said, "the whole forest will lose its colour."

They ran between the trees. Bright pink candyfloss flowers were the colour of smoke. The bell flowers' crimson petals were the colour of ashes.

Goldie's tail went limp, and she stopped. "The flowers have gone grey already," she said tearfully.

Jess hugged her. "We've defeated Grizelda before," she said firmly. "We'll do it again."

But Goldie's shoulders still slumped beneath her scarf.

"We'll fix it," Lily said. "Won't we, Layla?"

The meerkat nodded, but couldn't

manage a smile.

"I've never seen Goldie so down before," whispered Lily. "Even Layla has gone quiet. What do you think is happening?"

Jess pointed at the trees. "Everything in the forest is dull and miserable," she said. "It must be making the animals feel that way, too. Remember how sad all

the animals in Professor Cutiepaws's class were?"

"If we can't fix it," Lily said, following Layla through the grey puddles, "the animals will never be happy again, so they'll have to leave."

Goldie and Layla held paws as they walked between the greying trees. The girls followed them up a low grey hill studded with grey toadstools. As they walked, Goldie's scarf turned from shimmering gold to grey, and Layla's satchel did too.

Jess glanced down at her clothes. She and Lily were still dressed in bright colours.

"I think we'll be OK, because we don't live in the forest," she said. "But all the animals must be so worried about what's happening."

They arrived at a grey door in a grey tree trunk.

"This is my house," said Layla. She opened the door and the girls and Goldie followed Layla down twisting stairs into a room with grey walls and furnishings. Even the flames in the fireplace burned grey.

Layla's dad sat huddled in a grey woolly jacket with five meerkat pups, all

 55

snuggled in grey blankets.

"Layla!" said her dad. "Thank goodness you're home. Something dreadful's happening!"

"We think Grizelda's doing it," said Layla sadly. "Goldie, Jess and Lily are trying to help us."

"We'll fix this!" said Lily.

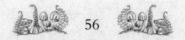

Layla's chin lifted just a bit, and she nodded.

The friends said a quick hello, then Layla showed them her collection of Madame Doodleflap's paintings. They were grey now too, but still very beautiful.

As Jess studied the paintings, she noticed a sparkling pond in several of them. Strange waterlilies floated on top. "These look so real," she said.

The petals seemed to dance in the breeze.

"The waterlily petals are really moving!" said Lily.

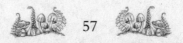

Mr Brighteye glanced up. "That's one of Madame Doodleflap's most magical paintings," he said. "The flowers are Winged Waterlilies. They only grow in Dewdrop Glade, near Sunshine Meadow."

Jess clapped her hands. "Madame Doodleflap must have been to Dewdrop Glade if she painted it. She must live nearby. Let's go!"

The girls and Goldie rushed to the stairs. But Layla darted in front of them.

"Wait!" cried Layla. "There's a much quicker way!"

CHAPTER FIVE

Dewdrop Glade

"A quicker way?" said Lily. "I thought Goldie knew all the forest paths."

"Our family has tunnels all over the forest," said Mr Brighteye. "Tunnels are quicker, because you don't have to go around trees or up and down hills." He rolled up three of Madame Doodleflap's pictures. "Take these," he said to Jess. "They might help. Good luck, everyone!"

The girls and Goldie followed Layla to a round room with ten tunnels leading from it.

"How can you tell which tunnel goes where?" Jess asked.

Layla showed them some faded paintings over each entrance. The first was of Mrs Longwhiskers the rabbit.

"So this tunnel goes to the Toadstool Café!" said Lily. "That's clever!"

"They're lovely paintings," said Jess, "even without colour."

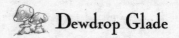

Layla cracked a small smile. "I did them."

"Wow!" said Lily. "You're so talented!"

"Thanks!" Layla showed them a painting of water droplets glistening on grass. "This way for Dewdrop Glade!"

"We're sure to find something to help us there," said Jess, giving Goldie a squeeze. "The colours will be back in no time!"

Goldie nodded. "You're right," she said.

Lily gave Jess a thumbs up. She could tell Layla and Goldie were starting to cheer up.

Layla led them through the long,

straight tunnel until they reached a grey
door. She opened it and they stepped out
into Dewdrop Glade.

Jess gazed at the dreary pond. "This
should be full of colour," she said.

Lily examined the bushes, where each
grey leaf and petal was sprinkled with
dewdrops. But they weren't sparkling
green or dazzling like diamonds, they

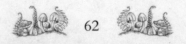

were dull and grey.

Goldie pointed to a pond. "There are the Winged Waterlilies," she cried. "This is the scene from the painting!"

"So Madame Doodleflap might live near here!" said Layla.

Jess and Lily searched around the pond for signs of Madame Doodleflap's home. Layla was helping Goldie check around

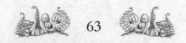

the edges of the glade when she suddenly let out a squeal. "Look!"

The others ran over and looked down on a tree stump speckled with spots of red, purple and yellow.

"It looks like splashes of paint," said Layla, peering closely. "But why isn't it grey like the rest of the forest?"

"It must be Madame Doodleflap's paint," Lily said excitedly. "Her paintings are magical, aren't they? So her paint hasn't lost its colour."

Jess's eyes shone. "The splashes of paint could lead us to her!"

They followed the paint trail out of a gloomy Dewdrop Glade, into a copse of grey Twisty Willow trees. The paint splatters stood out in the grey. But here the paint trail ended. There wasn't a home in sight.

"What do we do now?" said Goldie. She leaned against a tree trunk. Jess frowned in thought as she unrolled

the paintings they'd brought. Lily picked
a sniffling Layla up for a cuddle. Nobody
spoke for a moment.

"I've got it!" said Jess suddenly. "Look!
These pictures are all painted from above.
Maybe Madame Doodleflap climbs up
trees to paint."

"Of course! She's obviously shy," said
Lily, "and no one would see her if she hid
in a tree."

They all looked up, searching the
treetops. Then Jess spotted a flash of colour
in the greyness, high in a Twisty Willow.
"What's that?"

"I'll look," said Goldie. She scrambled up the tree trunk and stopped, peering up through the tangled branches.

"There's something big and bright up here," she said, pulling branches aside. "It looks like – a giant nest!"

Layla squealed. "Perhaps it's Madame Doodleflap's home!"

She scrambled after Goldie, with Jess and Lily following. The trunk was tall, but the twisting branches made perfect handholds so the tree was easy to climb.

A huge nest came into view. It was made of woven branches, painted blue

and yellow, and it spread across the
treetop. There was a sky-blue door and
the yellow knocker was sun-shaped.

"It must be where Madame Doodleflap
lives," said Jess. "It's still so colourful."

Goldie knocked on the door.

A surprised squawk came from inside.
"Who's there? I never have visitors!"

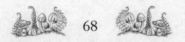

"Madame Doodleflap?" Jess called.

Silence.

Lily tried next. "Sorry if you're busy, Madame Doodleflap. But we need your help!"

There was a long pause.

"I'm afraid you've made a mistake," squawked the voice. "I'm just an ordinary bird. I can't help you."

Layla's head hung so low that Lily scooped her up and hugged her.

"It's hopeless," said Goldie.

"Please, Madame Doodleflap!" Layla called tearfully. "Only you can help!

You're my favourite artist and I so, so, so want to meet you!"

Silence again.

Then they heard the latch lift.

Excitement buzzed through Lily and Jess as, very slowly, the door began to open …

CHAPTER SIX

Magical Paint

Standing in the doorway was a beautiful red, blue and yellow parrot. She wore an indigo beret.

"Oh my," the parrot said shyly. "Look at all these visitors."

"Madame Doodleflap!" cried Layla. "Is it really you?"

 71

The parrot looked startled. Jess and Lily saw she was wearing a paint-splattered apron.

"It must be you," cried Lily.

The parrot blushed and nodded slowly. "Yes," she said. "I'm Madame Doodleflap."

Layla jumped forward and hugged the parrot, squeezing her tight in excitement.

Madame Doodleflap looked startled. Then she gently folded her wings around the little meerkat.

The girls and Goldie glanced at each other and smiled.

"Goodness!" Madame Doodleflap squawked. She was looking over Layla, into the forest. "The trees have turned grey!"

"That's why we're here," said Goldie. "Can we come in?"

Madame Doodleflap's wings fluttered anxiously. "Ooh, um, I don't usually have visitors. They'd make me stop and talk. And I just want to paint."

"We'll never tell anyone where you live, we promise," said Jess.

Layla put her paws together, begging, "Please, please, please?"

"All right," said Madame Doodleflap. "Come into my studio."

Inside, Goldie and the girls sat on scarlet and blue cushions. Layla darted around, examining the paints, brushes and half-finished pictures strewn across the wooden tables.

Jess showed Madame Doodleflap the book and explained what had happened.

The parrot turned the pages with a

wingtip, then closed the book. "This is terrible," she agreed. "But how can I help?"

"Could you paint the pictures again?" asked Lily. "It's the only way to bring the colour back."

Madame Doodleflap looked thoughtful. "It will take a very long time to do that –

unless I have help."

Layla scurried to her. "I'll help!" she cried. "I will, I will, I will! Please?"

Madame Doodleflap fluttered her wingtips. "Well then – I suppose – yes, of course you can help. Of course I will do it!"

She took a tray of glass paint pots from a cupboard.

Jess read the labels. "Lilac Laughter ... Good Luck Green ... Lavender Lullaby ... Crimson Cuddle ... What lovely names!"

"I think them up as I watch animals

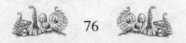

playing," Madame Doodleflap said.
"Here's Scarlet Smiles—"

Layla's eyes went wide. "You make
your own paints?"

Madame Doodleflap nodded. "I mix
strands from my own feathers with a
touch of white and a dab of black." She
set some dishes on a table. "I must mix
some now. Who's ready to help?"

"Me!" everyone cried.

Madame Doodleflap handed Layla a
tiny pair of golden scissors, shaped like
crossed feathers. She spread her wings.

 77

"Could you snip some strands from my red feathers?"

Layla's nose trembled as she held the scissors in her little paw. "Will it hurt you?"

"Not at all," said Madame Doodleflap. She gave Lily a tiny white dish to hold

beneath the feather to catch the strands.

Snip!

"Perfect!" said the parrot. "Now this blue feather."

Snip!

When they were done, Madame Doodleflap fetched a tall jug. As she took off the lid, a shimmering rainbow-coloured cloud formed around the top. She poured thick, clear liquid into the dish.

"This is magical paint," she explained. "Layla, tip the red and blue feather snippets into it."

Layla did so. Everyone stared, astonished, as the liquid changed colour.

Madame Doodleflap smiled. "That's Party Purple."

"Wow! Can we mix some?" asked Lily.

"Of course," said Madame Doodleflap. "I'll need lots of colours."

With the parrot's help, Goldie mixed a Rocking Red for the Toadstool Café's roof. Layla stirred white into red to make Pat-a-Cake Pink for roses. Lily added white to deep blue to make the colour of the Friendship Forest sky.

Jess struggled with blue and yellow to mix the exact green of the Treasure Tree, until Madame Doodleflap suggested a

touch more blue, and a speck of black.

"Perfect!" said Jess.

Madame Doodleflap began to paint. Her brush dabbed, stroked and flicked and, in minutes, Sunshine Meadow appeared on the page.

The friends stared, amazed.

"We're actually watching Madame Doodleflap paint!" Layla said in a hushed voice.

Madame Doodleflap was painting so fast her paint was running out.

"Let's mix more!" said Goldie.

They settled down to work, but froze

when they heard a sharp sound at the door.

Rap! Rap! Rap!

Madame Doodleflap leapt up, flapping anxiously. "Who's that?" she squawked. "No one else knows where I live!"

"Someone must have followed us," said Jess.

Rap! Rap! Rap!

Madame Doodleflap's wings ruffled with worry. "I'll suppose I should peep out to see who's there," she said.

She unlatched the door and it burst open. She squawked in fright as Gonzo flew in with a great flapping of wings.

"What do you want?" Goldie cried.

"I'm not letting you stop Grizelda's
spell!" Gonzo croaked.

To everyone's horror, he flew to the
open book and grabbed it!

CHAPTER SEVEN

Gorgeous Gonzo

Gonzo flew around the studio, clutching the book and laughing.

Everyone tried to grab the book, but he flew too high. "Can't catch me!" he croaked.

Layla scampered on to the work bench and leapt into the air, snatching at the

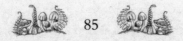

book as Gonzo whizzed past. But she wasn't strong enough to pull it free.

"It's hopeless," Lily said, lifting her down.

"Our poor forest!" Madame Doodleflap said, horrified. "What can we do?"

"Nothing!" croaked Gonzo. He was enjoying taunting them.

But Lily had an idea. "Do you remember," she whispered to Jess, "how

Gonzo said the class at Spelltop School should paint him because he's the most handsome creature in the forest?"

"I remember," said Jess.

Lily cleared her throat. "Gonzo," she called. "You really are handsome!"

"I know," the bird squawked.

"In fact," Lily went on, "you're so handsome that Jess wants to paint your portrait."

Gonzo slowed a little. "Really?" he croaked.

"Really!" Jess said, smiling at Lily. "Then you could look at it whenever you wanted."

He circled down and perched on a chair back. "All right. You can paint my portrait."

"I will," said Jess. "But you'll have to put down the book and keep very still."

Gonzo's feathers ruffled slightly as he thought. "I can keep still," he said finally, passing the book to Madame Doodleflap.

Everyone breathed a sigh of relief.

"You can start painting now," Gonzo
said to Jess.

"Say please," said Layla.

Gonzo hesitated. "Please," he said.

Lily helped him pose. "Leg to the side,"
she said. 'One wing curved. Tilt your head
to the left."

While Jess began painting Gonzo,
Madame Doodleflap continued
repainting the pictures in the book. Goldie
made rosehip tea and jam toasties for
everyone, and Layla studied every move
Madame Doodleflap made.

After a while, Jess whispered to the
parrot. "I've finished. What about you?"

"A few more brushstrokes …" Madame
Doodleflap replied.

"It's ready, Gonzo," said Jess.

The flamingo stretched his wings.
"Show me!" Layla gave him a stern look,
so he tried again. "Show me, please."

The painting showed Gonzo standing

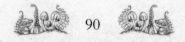

outside the Toadstool Café, with a lamb, a badger and other animals enjoying snacks nearby.

"You look gorgeous, Gonzo!" Lily said.

He nodded. "Like a king!"

Madame Doodleflap put down her brush. "The book's finished!"

Layla hugged her. "Thank you!"

"Let's see if it's worked," said Jess.

They all held their breath as Lily opened the door.

The sun peeped out from behind leafy trees … leafy green trees!

"It is working!" cried Layla.

The flowers glowed pink, yellow, purple and blue, and all the colours seemed brighter than ever. The four friends grasped hands and paws and danced around, cheering.

"Everything's beautiful!" cried Layla.

"And I feel like a weight's been lifted," said Goldie with a grin. "I'm so happy!"

Jess and Lily looked at each other in relief. The animals' spirits were up again!

They gathered around the parrot, hugging her.

"Thanks to you, Madame Doodleflap," said Lily, "we've done it!"

Jess grinned happily. "We've stopped Grizelda's spell and saved the forest!"

Gonzo was gazing at his portrait. "I wish I could paint," he said. "All I'm good at is being handsome."

Layla tapped Gonzo's knee. "I'm still learning to paint," she said. "You could learn, too!"

"Me?" Gonzo croaked.

"Yes!" said Layla.

Jess stroked Gonzo's

feathers. "It would be more fun than admiring yourself all day."

"And less lonely," said Lily. "You could paint other animals, like Layla, and make friends!"

"But how will I learn?" Gonzo asked.

Madame Doodleflap smiled. "I could teach you. We could have your first lesson right now!"

Gonzo was so thrilled he danced around the studio on his spindly legs.

"We'll take Layla back to school," said Jess. "Professor Cutiepaws will be wondering where we are!"

Madame Doodleflap waved goodbye
to the friends and took Layla's tiny paws
between her wingtips. "Come back soon,"
she said. "We'll have a painting picnic
together! Now you've shown me that
friends can be fun, I might like to meet
more animals." She smiled. "Perhaps one
day I could teach art at Spelltop School!"

Layla's smile stretched from cheek to
cheek.

Back in the forest, the colours were
fresh and bright, and butterflies fluttered
by, chattering joyfully in their tinkling
voices. Bright hummingbirds hovered

beside bell flowers, and milky-white starflowers gleamed in the sunlight.

Suddenly, Jess cried out. "Stop!"

An orb of yellow light was floating towards them.

"Grizelda!" said Lily. "Layla, stay back! She's going to be furious!"

CHAPTER EIGHT

Grizelda!

Grizelda was purple with rage. She screeched, "How dare you interfere!"

"We'll never let you have Friendship Forest!" Jess shouted.

"And how did you cast that spell, when you weren't at the school?" Lily yelled.

"By being clever!" Grizelda crowed.

"Not clever enough!" said Goldie.

"You wait!" Grizelda sneered. "I'll be back!" She snapped her fingers and vanished. But not before Jess caught sight of a tear in one sleeve of her black cloak ...

When the girls, Goldie and Layla

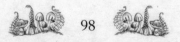

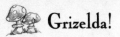

returned to Professor Cutiepaws's class, the animals erupted in cheers and applause. Soon, the school bluebell rang for lunch. Professor Gogglewing appeared with a big box from the Toadstool Café.

"Celebration cakes!" he said.

While everyone tucked into raspberry meringues, chocolate hazelnut puffs, peach tarts and strawberry cream cupcakes, Layla whispered something to Professor Gogglewing. He nodded. She took a cupcake and slipped indoors.

Lily looked up and saw Professor Cutiepaws walking over. She was frowning.

"I wonder what's wrong?" said Jess.

Before Lily could reply, a huge smile spread across Professor Cutiepaws's face. "Sweetiepies!" she cried. "Well done on saving the forest!"

"Thanks!" said Jess.

"Have a cake," said Lily.

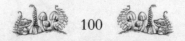

Professor Cutiepaws clapped her paws delightedly. "Oh, yummy yum-yums!" She bounced away to choose one.

When the bluebell rang again for afternoon lessons, the girls went to say goodbye to Layla.

"We have to go now," said Lily. She popped a kiss on Layla's head.

"Layla, show us your painting," said Professor Gogglewing.

Shyly, Layla turned the easel around. The girls gasped.

"It's a portrait of us!" said Jess.

The headmaster patted Layla's head.

"When it's
finished, we'll
hang it in
school to
remind us
of the day you all
saved Friendship Forest!"

"What a marvellous idea," said
Professor Cutiepaws. "I'll never forget
what our dear girlies did today, that's for
sure."

"Come back soon," said Layla. "Then
you'll see your portrait hanging up."

The girls promised they would, and said

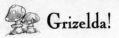

goodbye. Everyone waved as they set off through the forest with Goldie.

At the Friendship Tree, Goldie touched the trunk, and a door appeared.

"Promise you'll fetch us next time Grizelda causes trouble," said Lily.

Jess nodded. "Bye, Goldie."

The girls stepped through the doorway into golden light. They felt the tingle that meant they were returning to their proper size. When the light faded, they were back in Brightley Meadow. They ran back to Helping Paw together.

"Look, there are your painting things,"

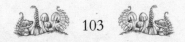

Lily said to Jess as they got back to the aviary. "You could finish painting Giggles."

"Let's both paint him!" said Jess.

"OK," said Lily.

Jess picked up her brush. "Thanks to Madame Doodleflap," she said, "I think I can mix the perfect shade of green now."

"Her paints had lovely names," said Lily. "What shall we call this one?"

They looked at each other and laughed. "Giggles Green, of course!"

The End

Join Lily and Jess at Spelltop School, where they learn all about the magic of Friendship Forest. But when lessons are disrupted by a mysterious spell, the girls must work together to find out what's happening.

Can gorgeous kitten Ava Fluffyface help them figure it out before it's too late?

Find out in the next Magic Animal Friends book,

Ava Fluffyface's Special Day

Turn over for a sneak peek ...

"What a beautiful speckled shell," said Lily Hart, gazing at the bird's egg in her hand.

"I've never seen such a pretty shade of blue," said her best friend, Jess Forester. She turned to Lily's mother. "Do you think it'll hatch, Mrs Hart?"

Mr and Mrs Hart were vets. They ran the Helping Paw Wildlife Hospital from the converted barn at the bottom of their garden. The girls were in the barn, showing Lily's mum their find. A curious little rabbit and a hedgehog with a hurt paw peered at them from hutches nearby.

Mrs Hart placed the egg in a box under a heat lamp. "There's a very good chance it'll hatch," she said. "It will be as warm as a nest in here."

"I can't wait!" declared Lily.

Lily and Jess loved helping with the animals, and the days when new babies were born were extra special.

"It's lucky you spotted the egg, Lily," said Jess.

"It was in the long grass next to the rescued guinea pigs," said Lily. "I think it fell from the apple tree there. I searched for the nest but I couldn't find it."

"I need to look at the lamb with the sore foot," said Mrs Hart. "I'll be back soon." She checked the heat lamp once more and went out.

Lily tucked her dark hair behind her ears and gazed at the egg on its soft bed. "What sort of bird will you be?" she whispered.

Suddenly they heard a miaow behind them.

A beautiful cat with golden fur and sparkling green eyes was sitting in the doorway.

"Goldie!" cried Jess.

The girls stroked Goldie's soft fur.
Goldie purred and rubbed happily against
their legs.

"This must mean we're off to
Friendship Forest!" cried Lily.

Read

Ava Fluffyface's Special Day

to find out what happens next!

Jess and Lily's Animal Facts

Lily and Jess love lots of different animals –
both in Friendship Forest
and in the real world.

Here are their top facts about

MEERKATS

like Layla Brighteye:

- On average meerkats are only 30 cm tall!
- They live in families of 20-50, in big underground burrows
- Meerkats normally have between two and four babies in a year. Other members of the meerkat family all help to babysit the babies!
- One meerkat, called a century, guards the meerkat family. It will stand on its back legs, propped up by its tail, and look out for danger while the rest of the family is above ground looking for food
- Meerkats have adapted to their desert homes by having dark patches around their eyes. This helps the meerkats to see through the bright sunshine
- Meerkats have very body little fat, so they have to forage and hunt every day

There's lots of fun for everyone at
www.magicanimalfriends.com

Play games and explore the secret world of
Friendship Forest, where animals can talk!

Join the
Magic Animal Friends Club!

⭐ Special competitions ⭐

⭐ Exclusive content ⭐

⭐ All the latest Magic Animal Friends news! ⭐

To join the Club, simply go to

www.magicanimalfriends.com/join-our-club/